Philip Roth

The Breast

In 1997 Philip Roth won the Pulitzer Prize for *American Pastoral.* In 1998 he received the National Medal of Arts at the White House and in 2002 the highest award of the American Academy of Arts and Letters, the Gold Medal in Fiction. He twice won the National Book Award and the National Book Critics Circle Award. He won the PEN/Faulkner Award three times. In 2005 *The Plot Against America* received the Society of American Historians' Prize for "the outstanding historical novel on an American theme for 2003–2004." Roth received PEN's two most prestigious awards: in 2006 the PEN/Nabokov Award and in 2007 the PEN/Bellow Award for achievement in American fiction. In 2011 he received the National Humanities Medal at the White House and was later named the fourth recipient of the Man Booker International Prize. He died in 2018.

BOOKS BY PHILIP ROTH

ZUCKERMAN BOOKS

The Ghost Writer
Zuckerman Unbound
The Anatomy Lesson
The Prague Orgy

The Counterlife

American Pastoral
I Married a Communist
The Human Stain

Exit Ghost

ROTH BOOKS

The Facts • Deception
Patrimony • Operation Shylock
The Plot Against America

KEPESH BOOKS

The Breast
The Professor of Desire
The Dying Animal

NEMESES: SHORT NOVELS

Everyman • Indignation
The Humbling • Nemesis

MISCELLANY

Reading Myself and Others
Shop Talk

OTHER BOOKS

Goodbye, Columbus • Letting Go
When She Was Good • Portnoy's Complaint • Our Gang
The Great American Novel • My Life as a Man
Sabbath's Theater

The Breast

Philip Roth

Vintage International
Vintage Books
A Division of Penguin Random House LLC
New York

FIRST VINTAGE INTERNATIONAL EDITION, MARCH 1994

The Library of Congress has cataloged the Knopf edition as follows:
Roth, Philip.
The breast / Philip Roth.—1st Vintage International ed.
p. cm.
1. College teachers—United States—Fiction.
2 . Metamorphosis—Fiction. 3. Breast—Fiction. I. Title.
PS3568.O855B7 1994
813'.54—dc20 93-43498

Vintage International Trade Paperback ISBN: 978-0-679-74901-1

www.vintagebooks.com

146086900

To Elizabeth Ames,
executive director of Yaddo
from 1924 to 1970,

and to
the Corporation of Yaddo,
Saratoga Springs, New York,

the best friends a writer could have

The Breast

It began oddly. But could it have begun otherwise, however it began? It has been said, of course, that everything under the sun begins oddly and ends oddly, and *is* odd. A perfect rose is "odd," so is an imperfect rose, so is the rose of ordinary rosy good looks growing in your neighbor's garden. I know about the perspective from which all that exists appears awesome and mysterious. Reflect upon eternity, consider, if you are up to it, oblivion, and everything becomes a wonder. Still, I would submit to you, in all humility, that some things are more wondrous than others, and that I am one such thing.

It began oddly—a mild, sporadic tingling in the groin. During that first week I would retire several times a day to the men's room adjacent to my office in the humanities building to take down my trousers, but upon examining myself, I saw nothing out of the ordinary, assiduous as was my search. I decided, halfheartedly, to ignore it. I had been so devout a hypochondriac all my life, so alert to every change in body temperature and systemic regularity, that the reasonable man I also was had long found it impossible to take seriously all my telltale symptoms. Despite the grim premonitions of extinction or paralysis or unendurable pain that accompanied each new ache or fever, I was, at thirty-eight, a man of stamina and appetite, six feet tall with good posture and a trim physique, most of my hair and all of my teeth, and no history of major illness. Though I might rush to identify this tingling in my groin with some neurological disease on the order of shingles—if not worse—I simultaneously understood that it was undoubtedly, as always, nothing.

I was wrong. It was something. Another week passed before I discerned a barely perceptible pinkening of the skin beneath the pubic hair, a blemish so faint, however, that I finally instructed myself to stop looking; it was no more than a minor irritation and certainly nothing to worry about. After another week—making, for the record, an incubation period of twenty-one days—I glanced down one evening while stepping into the shower and discovered that through the hectic day of teaching and conferences and commuting and dining out, the flesh at the base of my penis had turned a shade of pale red. Dye, I instantly decided, from my undershorts. (That the undershorts at my feet were light blue meant nothing in that panic-stricken burst of disbelief.) I looked *stained*, as though something—a berry of some sort—had been crushed against my pubes and the juices had run down onto my member, raggedly coloring the root.

In the shower I lathered and rinsed my penis and pubic hair three times, then coated myself carefully from thighs to navel with a thick icing of soap bubbles that I proceeded to massage into my flesh for a count of sixty; when I rinsed with hot water—burning hot this time—the stain was still there. Not a rash, not a scab, not a bruise or a sore, but a deep pigment change that I associated at once with cancer.

It was just midnight, the time when transformations routinely take place in horror stories—and a hard hour to get a doctor in New York. Nonetheless, I immediately telephoned my physician, Dr. Gordon, and despite an attempt to hide my alarm, he heard the fear easily enough and volunteered to dress and come across town to examine me. Perhaps if Claire had been with me that night instead of back at her own apartment preparing a curriculum-committee report, I would have had the courage of my terror and told the doctor to come running. Of course on the basis of my symptoms at that hour it is unlikely that Dr. Gordon would have rushed me then and there into a hospital, nor does it appear from what we now know—or continue not to know—that anything could have been done in the hospital to prevent or arrest what was under way. The agony of the next four hours I was to spend alone might perhaps have been alleviated by morphine, but nothing indicates that the course of the disaster could have been reversed by any medical procedure short of euthanasia.

With Claire at my side I might have been able

to cave in completely, but alone I suddenly felt ashamed of losing control; it was no more than five minutes since I'd discovered the stain, and there I was, wet and nude on my leather sofa, trying vainly to overcome the tremolo in my voice as I looked down and described into the phone what I saw. *Take hold*, I thought—and so I took hold, as I can when I tell myself to. If it was what I feared, it could wait until morning; if it wasn't, it could also wait. I would be fine, I told the doctor. Exhausted from a hard day's work, I had just been—startled. I would see him in his office at—I thought this brave of me—about noon. Nine, he said. I agreed and, calmly as I could, said good night.

Not until I hung up and examined myself yet again under a strong light did I remember that there was a third symptom—aside from the tingling groin, and the discolored penis—that I had failed to mention to the doctor; I had taken it, until that moment, for a sign of health rather than of disease. This was the intensity of local sensation I had experienced at sex with Claire during the preceding three weeks. To me it had signaled the resurgence of my old desire for her; from where or why I did not even care to question, so thrilled—and so relieved—was I to have it back. As it was, the strong lust her physical beauty had aroused in me during the first two years of our affair had been dwindling for almost a year now. Until lately, I would make love to her no more than two or three times a month and, more often than not, at her provocation.

My cooling down—my coldness—was distressing to both of us, but as we both had endured enough emotional upheaval in our lives (she as a child with her parents, I as an adult with my wife), we were equally reluctant to take any steps toward dissolving our union. Dispiriting as it surely was for a lovely and voluptuous young woman of twenty-five to be spurned night after night, Claire displayed outwardly none of the suspicion or frustration or anger that would have seemed justified even to me, the source of her unhappiness. Yes, she pays a price for this equanimity—she is not the most expressive woman I have ever known, for all her sexual passion—but I have reached the stage in my life—that is, I *had*—where the calm harbor and its placid waters were more to my liking than the foaming drama of the high seas. Of course there were times—out in company, or sometimes just alone over our dinner—when I might have wished her livelier and more responsive, but I was far too content with her dependable sobriety to be disappointed in her for lacking color. I had had enough color, thank you, with my wife.

Indeed, during the course of three years, Claire and I had worked out a way of living together—which in part entailed living separately—that provided us the warmth and security of each other's affections, without the accompanying dependence, or the grinding boredom, or the wild, unfocused yearning, or the round-the-clock strategies of deception and placation which seemed to have soured all but a very few of the marriages we knew. A year back I had ended five years of psychoanalysis convinced that the wounds sustained in my own Grand Guignol marriage had healed as well as they ever would, and in large part because of my life with Claire. Maybe I wasn't the man I'd been, but I wasn't a bleeding buck private any longer, either, wrapped in bandages and beating the drum of self-pity as I limped tearfully into the analyst's office from that battlefield known as Hearth and Home. Life had become orderly and stable—the first time I could say that in more than a decade. We really did get on so easily and with so little strain, we liked each other so much that it seemed to me something very like a disaster (little I knew about disaster) when, out of the blue, I began to take no pleasure at all in our lovemaking. It was a depressing, bewildering development, and try as I might, I seemed unable to alter it. I was, in fact, scheduled to pay a visit to my former analyst to talk about how much this was troubling me, when, out of the blue again, I was suddenly more passionate with her than I had ever been with anyone.

But "passion" is the wrong word: an infant in the crib doesn't feel passion when it delights in being tickled playfully under the chin. I am talking about purely tactile delight—sex neither in the head nor the heart, but excruciatingly in the epidermis of the penis, sex skin-deep and ecstatic. It was a kind of pleasure that made me writhe and claw at the sheets, made me twist and turn in the bed with a helpless abandon that I had previously associated more with women than with men—and women more imaginary than real. During the final week of my incubation period, I nearly cried with *tears* from the sheer tortuous pleasure of the friction alone. When I came I took Claire's ear in my mouth and licked it like a dog. I licked her hair. I found myself panting, licking my own shoulder. I had been saved! My life with Claire had been spared! Having lain indifferently beside her for nearly a year, having begun to fear the worst about our future, I had somehow—blessed mysterious somehow!—found my way to a pure, primitive realm of erotic susceptibility where the bond between us could only be strengthened. "Is this what is meant by debauchery?" I asked my happy friend whose pale skin bore the marks of my teeth; "it's like nothing I've ever known." She only smiled, and closed her eyes to float a little more. Her hair was stringy with perspiration, like a little girl's from playing too long in the heat. Pleasured, pleasure-giving Claire. Lucky David. We couldn't have been happier.

Alas, what has happened to me is like nothing *anyone* has ever known: beyond understanding, beyond compassion, beyond comedy. To be sure, there are those who claim to be on the very brink of a conclusive scientific explanation; and those, my faithful visitors, whose compassion is seemingly limitless; and then, out in the world, those—why shouldn't there be?—who cannot help laughing. And, you know, at times I am even one with them: I understand, I have compassion, I too see the joke. Enjoying it is another matter. If only I could sustain the laughter for more than a few seconds—if only it weren't so brief and so bitter. But then maybe more laughs are what I have to look forward to, if the medical men are able to sustain life in me in this condition, and if I should continue to want them to.

I am a breast. A phenomenon that has been variously described to me as "a massive hormonal influx," an "endocrinopathic catastrophe," and/or "a hermaphroditic explosion of chromosomes" took place within my body between midnight and 4 a.m. on February 18, 1971, and converted me into a mammary gland disconnected from any human form, a mammary gland such as could only appear, one would have thought, in a dream or a Dali painting. They tell me that I am now an organism with the general shape of a football, or a dirigible; I am said to be of spongy consistency, weighing one hundred and fifty-five pounds (formerly I was one hundred and sixty-two), and measuring, still, six feet in length. Though I continue to retain, in damaged and "irregular" form, much of the cardiovascular and central nervous systems, an excretory system described as "reduced and primitive," and a respiratory system that terminates just above my mid-section in something resembling a navel with a flap, the basic architecture in which these human characteristics are disarranged and buried is that of the breast of the mammalian female.

The bulk of my weight is fatty tissue. At one end I am rounded off like a watermelon, at the other I terminate in a nipple, cylindrical in shape, projecting five inches from my "body" and perforated at the tip with seventeen openings, each about half the size of the male urethral orifice. These are the apertures of the lactiferous ducts. As I am able to understand it without the benefit of diagrams—I am sightless—the ducts branch back into lobules composed of the sort of cells that secrete the milk that is carried to the surface of the normal nipple when it is being suckled, or milked by machine.

My flesh is smooth and "youthful," and I am still a "Caucasian." The color of my nipple is rosy pink. This last is thought to be unusual because in my former incarnation I was an emphatic brunet. As I told the endocrinologist who made this observation, I find it less unusual than certain other aspects of the transformation, but then I am not the endocrinologist around here. Embittered wit, but wit at last, and it must have been observed and noted.

My nipple is rosy pink—like the stain at the base of my penis the night this all happened to me. Since the apertures in the nipple provide me with something like a mouth and vestigial ears—at least it has seemed to me that I am able to make myself heard through my nipple, and, faintly, to hear through it what is going on around me—I had assumed that it was my head that had become my nipple. But the doctors conclude otherwise, at least as of this month. For one thing, my voice, faint as it is, evidently emanates from the flap in my mid-section, even if my sense of internal landscape doggedly continues to associate the higher functions of consciousness with the body's topmost point. The doctors now maintain that the wrinkled, roughened skin of the nipple—

which, admittedly, is exquisitely sensitive to touch like no tissue on the face, including the mucous membrane of the lips—was formed out of the glans penis. That puckered pinkish areola encircling the nipple is said to have metamorphosed from the shaft of the penis under the assault of a volcanic secretion from the pituitary of "mammogenic" fluid. Two fine long reddish hairs extend from one of the small elevations on the rim of my areola. "How long are they?"

"Seven inches exactly."

"My antennae." The bitterness. Then the disbelief. "Will you pull one, please?"

"If you like, David, I'll pull very gently."

Dr. Gordon wasn't lying. A hair of mine had been tugged. A familiar enough sensation—indeed, so familiar that I wanted to be dead.

Of course it was days after the change—the "change"!—before I even regained consciousness, and another week after that before they would tell me anything other than that I had been "very ill" with "an endocrine imbalance." I keened and howled so wretchedly each time I awoke to discover anew that I could not see, smell, taste, or move that I had to be kept under heavy sedation. When my "body" was touched, I didn't know what to make of it: the sensation was unexpectedly soothing, but far away, it reminded me of water lapping at a beach. One morning I awakened to feel something new happening to me at one of my extremities. Nothing like pain—rather more like pleasure—yet it felt so strange just to *feel* that I screamed, "I've been burned! I was in a fire!"

"Calm yourself, Mr. Kepesh," a woman said. "I'm onlywashing you. I'm only washing your face."

"My face? Where is it! Where are my arms! My legs! Where is my mouth! *What happened to me?*"

Now Dr. Gordon spoke. "You're in Lenox Hill Hospital, David. You're in a private room on the seventh floor. You've been here ten days. I've been to see you every morning and night. You are getting excellent care and all the attention you require. Right now you're just being washed with a sponge and some warm soapy water. That's all. Does that hurt you?"

"No," I whimpered, "but where is my face?"

"Just let the nurse wash you, and we'll talk a little later in the morning. You must get all the rest you can."

"What happened to me?" I could remember the pain and the terror, but no more: to me it had felt as though I were being repeatedly shot from a cannon into a brick wall, then marched over by an army of boots. In actuality it was more as though I had been a man made of taffy, stretched in opposite directions by my penis and my buttocks until I was as wide as I had once been long. The doctors tell me that I couldn't have been conscious for more than a few minutes once the "catastrophe" got going, but in retrospect, it seems to me that I had been awake to feel every last bone in my body broken in two and ground into dust.

"If only you'll relax now—"

"How am I being fed!"

"Intravenously. You mustn't worry. You're being fed all you need."

"Where are my arms!"

"Just let the nurse wash you, and then she'll rub some oil in, and you'll feel much better. Then you can sleep."

I was awakened like this every morning, but it was another week or more before I was sufficiently calm—or torpid—to associate the sensations of washing with erotic excitement. By now I had concluded that I was a quadruple amputee—that the boiler had burst beneath the bedroom of my parlor-floor apartment, and I had been blinded and mutilated in the explosion. I sobbed almost continuously, giving no credence whatsoever to the hormonal explanations that Dr. Gordon and his colleagues proposed for my "illness." Then one morning, depleted and numb from my days of tearless weeping, I felt myself becoming aroused—a mild throbbing in the vicinity of what I still took to be my face, a pleasing feeling of . . . engorgement.

"Do you like that?" The voice was a man's! A stranger's!

"*Who are you? Where am I? What is going on?*"

"I'm the nurse."

"*Where's the other nurse!*"

"It's Sunday. Take it easy—it's only Sunday."

The next morning the regular nurse, Miss Clark, returned to duty, accompanied by Dr. Gordon. I was washed, under Dr. Gordon's supervision, and this time, when I began to experience the sensations that accompany erotic fondling, I let them envelop me. "Oh," I whispered, "that does feel nice."

"What is it?" asked Dr. Gordon. "What are you saying, David?"

The nurse began to rub in the oil. I could feel each one of her fingers kneading that face no longer a face. Then something began to make me tingle, something that I soon realized was only the soft palm of her hand slowly moving in caressing circles on that faceless face. My whole being was seething with that exquisite sense of imminence that precedes a perfect ejaculation. "Oh, my God, this is so wonderful." And then I began to sob so uncontrollably that I had to be put back to sleep.

Shortly thereafter, Dr. Gordon came with Dr. Klinger, who for five years had been my psychoanalyst, and they told me what it is I have become.

I was washed gently but thoroughly every morning and then smeared with oil and massaged. After I heard the truth about myself—after learning that I live now in a hammock, my nipple at one end, my rounded, bellied underside at the other, and with two velvet harnesses holding my bulk in place—it was several months before I could take even the remotest pleasure in these morning ablutions. And even then it was not until Dr. Gordon consented to leave me alone in the room with the nurse that I was again able to surrender wholly to Miss Clark's ministering fingers. But when I did, the palpations were almost more than could be borne, deliciously "almost"—a frenzy akin to what I had experienced in those final weeks of lovemaking with Claire, but even more extreme, it seemed, coming to me in my state of utter helplessness, and out of nothingness, and from this source dedicated solely to kindling my excitement. When the session was over and Miss Clark had retired from my room with her basin of warm water and the vials of oil (I imagined colored vials), my hammock would sway comfortingly to and fro, until at last my heaving stopped, my nipple softened, and I slept the sleep of the sated.

I say the doctor consented to leave us alone in the room. But how do I know anyone has ever left me alone, or that this is even a room? Dr. Gordon assures me that I am under no more surveillance than any other difficult case—I am not on display in a medical amphitheater, am not being exposed to closed-circuit television . . . but what's to prevent him from lying? I doubt that in the midst of this calamity anybody is watching out for my civil liberties. That *would* be laughable. And why do I even care if I am not alone when I think I am? If I am under a soundproof glass dome on a platform in the middle of Madison Square Garden, if I am on display in Macy's window—what's the difference to me? Wherever they have put me, however many may be looking in at me, I am really quite as alone as anyone could ever wish to be. Best to stop thinking about my "dignity," regardless of all it meant to me when I was a professor of literature, a lover, a son, a friend, a neighbor, a customer, a client, and a citizen. If ever there was a time to forget about propriety, decorum, and personal pride, this is it. But as these are matters intimately connected to my idea of sanity and to my self-esteem, I am, in fact, troubled now as I wasn't at all in my former life, where the style of social constraint practiced by the educated classes came quite easily to me, and provided real satisfaction. Now the thought that my morning sessions with Miss Clark are being carried live on intra-hospital TV, that my delirious writhings are being observed by hundreds of scientists assembled in the galleries overhead . . . well, that is sometimes almost as unbearable as the rest of it. Nonetheless, when Dr. Gordon assures me that my "privacy" is being respected, I no longer contradict him. I say instead, "Thank you for that," and in this way I am able at least to pretend to them that I think I am alone even if I'm not.

You see, it is not a matter of doing what is right or seemly; I can assure you that I am not concerned with the etiquette of being a breast. Rather, it is doing what I must, to continue to be me. For if not me, who? Or what? Either I continue to be myself or I go mad—and then I die. And it seems I don't want to die. A surprise to me too, but there it is. I don't foresee a miracle either, some sort of retaliatory raid by my anti-mammogenic hormones, if such there be (and God alone knows if there are in someone made like me), that will undo the damage. I suspect it's a little late for that, and so it is not with this hope springing eternally in the human breast that the human breast continues to want to be. Human I insist I am, but not that human. Nor do I believe the worst is over. I get the feeling that the worst is yet to come. No, it is simply that having been terrified of death since the age of two, I have become entrenched in my hatred of it, have taken a personal stand *against* death from which I seem unable to retreat because of This. Horrible indeed This is; but on the other hand, I have been wanting not to die for so long now, I just can't stop doing it overnight. I need time.

That I have not died is, as you can imagine, of great interest to medical science. *That* miracle continues to be studied by microbiologists, physiologists, and biochemists working here in the hospital and, I am told, in medical institutions around the country. They are trying to figure out what makes me still tick. Dr. Klinger thinks that no matter how they put the puzzle together, in the end it could all come down to those old pulpit bromides, "strength of character" and "the will to live." And who am I not to concur in such a heroic estimate of myself?

"It appears then that my analysis has 'taken,'" I tell Dr. Klinger; "a tribute to you, sir." He laughs. "You were always stronger than you thought." "I would as soon never have had to find out. And besides it's not so. I can't live like this any longer." "Yet you have, you do." "I do *but I can't.* I was never strong. Only determined. One foot in front of the other. Good grades in all subjects. It goes back to handing homework in on time and carrying off the prizes. Dr. Klinger, *it's hideous in here.* I want to quit, I want to go crazy, to go spinning off, ranting and wild, *only I can't.* I sob. I scream. I touch bottom. I lie there on that bottom! But then I come around. I make my mordant little jokes. I listen to the radio. I listen to the phonograph. I think about what we've said. I restrain my rage and I restrain my misery—and I wait for your next visit. But this is madness, my coming around. To be putting one foot in front of the other is madness—*especially as I have no feet!* This ghastly thing has happened, and I listen to the six o'clock news! This incredible catastrophe, and

I listen to the weather report!" No, no, says Dr. Klinger: strength of character, the will to live.

I tell him that I want to go mad, he tells me that it's impossible: beyond me, *beneath* me. It took This for me to find that I am a citadel of sanity.

So—I may pretend otherwise, but I know they are studying me, watching as they would from a glass-bottomed boat the private life of a porpoise or a manatee. I think of these aquatic mammals because of the overall resemblance I now bear to them in size and shape, and because the porpoise in particular is said to be an intelligent, perhaps even rational, creature. Porpoise with a Ph.D. Associate Porpoise Kepesh. Oh, really, it is the silliness, the triviality, the *meaninglessness* of life that one misses most in a life like this. For quite aside from the monstrous, ludicrous fact of me, there is the intellectual responsibility that I seem to have developed to this preposterous misfortune. WHAT DOES IT MEAN? HOW COULD IT HAVE HAPPENED? IN THE ENTIRE HISTORY OF THE HUMAN RACE, WHY PROFESSOR KEPESH? Yes, it is clever of Dr. Klinger to keep to what is ordinary and familiar, to drone on about strength of character and the will to live. Better those banalities than the grandiose or the apocalyptic; for citadel of sanity though I may be, there is really only so much that even I can take.

As far as I know, my only visitors other than the scientists, the doctors, and the hospital staff, have been Claire, my father, and Arthur Schonbrunn, formerly my department chairman and now the Dean of Arts and Sciences. My father's behavior has been staggering. I don't know how to account for it, except to say that I simply never knew the man. Nobody knew the man. Aggressive, cunning, at his work tyrannical—with us, the little family, innocent, protective, tender, and deeply in love. But this self-possession face to face with such horror? Who would have expected it from the owner of a second-class South Fallsburg hotel? A short-order cook to begin with, he rose eventually to be the innkeeper himself; retired now, he "kills time" answering the phone mornings at his brother's booming catering service in Bayside. Once a week he comes to visit and, seated in a chair that is drawn up beside my nipple, tells me all the news about our former guests. Remember Abrams the milliner? Cohen the chiropodist? Remember Rosenheim with the card tricks and the Cadillac? Yes, yes, I think so. Well, this one is near death, this one has moved, this one's son has gone and married an Egyptian. "How do you like that?" he says; "I didn't even know they would allow that over there." It is an awesome performance. Only is it performance? Is he the world's most brilliant actor, or just a simpleton, or just completely numb? Or has he no choice other than to go on being himself? *But doesn't he get what has happened? Doesn't the man understand that some things are more unusual even than a Jew marrying an Egyptian?*

One hour, and then he leaves for home—without kissing me. Something new for my father, leaving without that kiss. And that is when I realize he is no simpleton. It is a performance—and my father is a great and brave and noble man.

And my excitable mother? Mercifully for her she is dead; if she weren't, this would have killed her. Or am I wrong about her too? She put up with alcoholic bakers and homicidal salad men and bus boys who still wet the bed—so who knows, maybe she could have put up with me too. *Beasts*, she called them, *barnyard animals*, but always she went back to the kettles, back to the cleanser and the mops and the linens, despite the *angst* she endured from Memorial Day weekend to Yom Kippur because of the radical imperfection of our help. Isn't it from my mother that I learned determination to begin with? Isn't it from her example that I learned how one goes on from summer to winter to summer again, in spite of everything? So, still more banality: I am able to bear being a mammary gland because of my upbringing in a typically crisis-ridden Catskill hotel.

Claire, whose equanimity has from the first been such a tonic to me, a soothing antidote to the impulsiveness of my former wife, and I suppose even to my mother's palpitations and all the hotel-kitchen crises—Claire, oddly, was not nearly so good as my father at quelling her anguish right off. What was astonishing wasn't her tears, however, but the weight of her head on my midsection when she broke down and began to sob. *Her face on this flesh? How can she touch me?* I had been expecting never to be handled again by anyone other than the medical staff. I thought, "If Claire had become a penis . . ." But that was just too ridiculous to contemplate—inasmuch, that is, as it hadn't happened. Besides, what had happened to me had happened to me and no one else because it could not happen to anyone else, and even if I did not know why that was so, it was so, and there must be reasons to make it so, whether I was ever to know them or not. Perhaps, as Dr. Klinger observed, putting myself in Claire's shoes was somewhat beyond the call of duty. Perhaps; but if Claire *had* become a five-foot-nine-inch male member, I doubt that I would be capable of such devotion.

It was only a few days after her first visit that Claire consented to massage my nipple. Had she wept from a safe distance, I could never have been so quick to make the suggestion; I might never have made it at all. But the very moment I felt the weight of her head touch down upon me, *all* the possibilities opened up in my mind, and it was only a matter of time (and not very much of that) before I dared to ask for the ultimate act of sexual grotesquerie, in the circumstances.

I must make clear, before going further, that Claire is no vixen; though throughout our affair she had been wonderfully aroused by ordinary sexual practices, she had no taste, for instance, for intercourse *per anum*, and was even squeamish about receiving my sperm in her mouth. If she performed fellatio at all, it was only as a brief antecedent to intercourse, and never with the intention of bringing me off. I did not complain bitterly about this, but from time to time, as men who have not yet been turned into breasts are wont to do, I registered my discontent—I was not, you see, getting all I wanted out of life.

Yet it was Claire who suggested that she would play with my nipple if that was what I most desired.

This was during her fourth visit in four days. I had described to her for the first time how the nurse ministered to me in the mornings. I planned—for the time being anyway—to say this and no more.

But Claire immediately asked, "Would you like me to do what she does?"

"Would you—do that?"

"Of course, if you want me to."

Of course. Cool, imperturbable girl!

"I do!" I cried. "Please, I do!"

"You tell me what you like then," she said. "You tell me what feels best."

"Claire, is anyone else in the room?"

"No, no—just you and me."

"Is this being televised, Claire?"

"Oh, sweetheart, no, of course it isn't."

"Oh, then squeeze me, squeeze me hard!"

Once again, days later, after I made incoherent conversation about my nurse for nearly an hour, Claire said, "David dearest, what is it? Do you want my mouth?"

"Yes, yes!"

How could she? How can she? Why does she? Would *I*? I say to Dr. Klinger, "It's too much to ask. It's too awful. I have to stop this. I want her to do it all the time, every minute she's here.

I don't want to talk any more. I don't want her to read to me—I don't even listen. I just want her to squeeze me and suck me and lick me. I can't get enough of it. I can't stand it when she stops. I shout, I scream, "Go on! More! Go on!" But I'll drive her away, I will, I know, if I don't stop. And then I'll have no one. Then I'll have the nurse in the morning—and that's all I'll have. My father will come and tell me who died and who got married. And you will come and tell me about my strong character and my will to live. *But I won't have a woman!* I won't have Claire or sex or love ever again! I don't want to drive her away, it's bizarre enough now—but I want her clothes off, all of them off, at her feet, on the floor. I want her to get up on me and *roll* on me. Oh, Doctor, I want to fuck her! With my nipple! But if I even say it, it will drive her away! She'll run and never return!"

Claire visits every evening after dinner. During the day she teaches fourth grade at the Bank Street School here in New York. She is a Phi Beta Kappa graduate of Cornell; her mother is principal of a school in Schenectady, divorced now from her father, an engineer with Western Electric. Her older sister is married to an economist in the Commerce Department, and lives with him and four little children in Alexandria, Virginia. They own a house on the South Beach of Martha's Vineyard, where Claire and I visited them on our way to a week's vacation in Nantucket last summer. We argued politics—the Vietnam war. That done, we played fly-catcher-up with the kids down on the beach and then went off to eat boiled lobsters in Edgartown; afterward we sat in the movies, big, hearty, hairy carnivores, reduced in the cozy dark to nothing more than wind-burned faces and buttered fingers. Delicious. We had a fine time, really, "square" as were our hosts—I know they were square because they kept telling me so. Yet we had such a good time. She is something to look at on the beach, a green-eyed blonde, tall and lean and full-breasted. Even with desire on the wane, I still liked nothing better than to lie in bed and watch her dress in the morning and undress at night. Down in the hollow of the dunes, I unclip the top of her bikini and watch it drop away. "Imagine," she says, "where they'll be at fifty, if they droop like this at twenty-five." "Can't," I say, "won't," and drawing her to her knees, I lean back on the hot sand, dig down with my heels, shut my eyes, and wait with open lips for her breast to fill my mouth. Oh, what a sensation, there with the sea booming below! As though it were the globe itself—suckable soft globe!—and I Poseidon or Zeus! Oh, nothing beats the pleasures of the anthropomorphic god. "Let's spend all next summer by the ocean," I say, as people do on the first happy day of vacation. Claire whispers, "First let's go home and make love." It's been some time—she's right. "Oh, let's just lie here," I say—"Where is that strange thing? Oh, again, again." "I don't want to cut off your air. You were turning green." "With envy," I say.

Yes, I admit openly, that is what I said. And if this were a fairy tale instead of my life, we would have the moral now: "Beware preposterous desires—you may get lucky." But as this is decidedly *not* some fairy tale—not to me, dear reader—why should a wish like that have been the one to come true? I assure you that I have wanted things far less whimsically in my life than I wanted on that beach to be breasted. Why should playful, loverly words—spoken on the first day of our idyllic vacation!—become flesh, while whatever I have wanted in deadly earnest I have been able to achieve, if at all, only by putting one foot in front of the other over the course of thirty-eight years? No, I refuse to surrender my bewilderment to the wish-fulfillment theory. Neat and fashionable and delightfully punitive though it may be, I refuse to believe that I am this thing because this is a thing that I wanted to be. No! Reality is just a little grander than that. Reality has *some* style.

There. For those who prefer a fairy tale to life, a moral: "Reality," concludes the embittered professor who for reasons unbeknown to himself became a female breast, "has style." Go, you sleek, self-satisfied Houyhnhnms to whom nothing disgusting has yet happened, go and moralize on that!

It was not to Claire that I made my "grotesque" proposal then, but to my female nurse. I said, "Do you know what I think about when you wash me like this? Can I tell you what I am thinking about right now?"

"What is that, Professor Kepesh?"

"I would like to fuck you with my nipple."

"Can't hear you, Professor."

"I get so excited I want to fuck you! I want you to sit on my nipple—with your cunt!"

"I'll be finished with you now in just a moment . . ."

"*Did you hear me, whore? Did you hear what I want?*"

"Just drying you down now . . ."

By the time Dr. Klinger arrived at four I was one hundred and fifty-five pounds of remorse. I even began to sob a little when I told him what I had done—against all my misgivings and despite his warning. Now, I said, it was recorded on tape; for all I knew, it would be on page one of tomorrow's tabloids. A light moment for the straphangers on their way to work. For there certainly was a humorous side to it all; what is a catastrophe without its humorous side? Miss Clark—as I had known all along—is a short, stocky spinster, fifty-six years old.

Unlike Dr. Gordon, Claire, and my father, who continually assure me that I am not being watched other than by those who announce their presence, Dr. Klinger has never even bothered to dispute the issue with me. "And? If it is on page one? What of it?"

"It's nobody's business!" Still weeping.

"But you certainly would like to do it, would you not?"

"Yes! Yes! But she ignored me! She pretended I'd asked her to hurry up and be done! I don't want her any more! I want a new nurse!"

"Have anyone in mind?"

"Someone young—someone beautiful! Why not!"

"Someone who will hear you and say yes."

"Yes! Why not! It's insane otherwise! I should have what I want! This is no ordinary life and I am not going to pretend that it is! *You* want me to be ordinary, you *expect* me to be ordinary—in this condition! I'm supposed to go on being a sensible, rational man—in this condition! But that is crazy of you, Doctor! I want her to sit on me with her cunt! And why not! I want Claire to do it! What makes that 'grotesque'? To be denied my pleasure in the midst of this—*that* is grotesque!

I want to be fucked! Why shouldn't I be fucked? Tell me why that shouldn't be! Instead you torture me! Instead you prevent me from having what I want! Instead I lie here being sensible! And there's the madness, Doctor—being sensible!"

I do not know how much of what I said Dr. Klinger even understood; it is difficult enough to follow me when I am speaking deliberately, with concentration, and now I was sobbing and howling with no regard for the TV cameras or the spectators up in the stands . . . Or is that *why* I was carrying on so? Was I really so racked by the proposal I'd made that morning to Miss Clark? Or was the display largely for the benefit of my great audience, to convince them that, appearances aside, I am still very much a man—for who but a man has conscience, reason, desire, and remorse?

This crisis lasted for months. I became increasingly lewd with the stout, implacable Miss Clark, until finally one morning I offered her money. "Bend over—take it from behind! I'll give you anything you want!" How I would get the money into her hands, how I would go about borrowing if she demanded more than I had saved in my account I tried to figure out during my long, empty days. Who would help me? I couldn't very well ask my father or Claire, and they were the only two people by whom I was willing to be seen. Ridiculous perhaps, given how sure I was that my image was being mercilessly recorded by television cameras and my daily progress publicized in the *Daily News*, but then I am not arguing that since my transformation I have been a model of Mature Adult Responsible Behavior. I am only trying to describe, as best I can, the stages I have had to pass through on the way to the present phase of melancholy equilibrium . . . Of course to assist me—to get hold of the money, to make the financial arrangements, either with Miss Clark, or, if need be, with some woman whose profession is not circumscribed by a nurse's ethical outlook—I could easily have called upon a young bearded colleague, a clever poet from Brooklyn who is no prude and whose sexual adventurousness has made him somewhat notorious in our English Department. But then neither was I a prude, and once upon a time I had had a taste for sexual adventure no less developed than my young friend's. You must understand that it was not a man of narrow experience and suffocating inhibitions who was being tormented by his desires in that hammock. I had experimented with whores easily enough back in my twenties, and during a year as a Fulbright student in London, I had for several months carried on a thrilling, overwrought affair with two young women—students my age on leave together from university in Sweden, who shared a basement bedroom with me—until the less stable of the pair tried halfheartedly to pitch herself under a lorry. No, what alarmed me wasn't the strangeness of my desires in that hammock, but the degree to which I would be severing myself from my own past—and kind—by surrendering to them. I was afraid that the further I went the further I would go—that I would reach a point of frenzy from which I would pass over into a state of being that no longer had anything to do with who or what I once had been. It wasn't even that I would no longer be myself—I would no longer be anyone. I would have become craving flesh and nothing more.

So, with Dr. Klinger's assistance, I set about

to extinguish—and if not to extinguish, at least (in Klinger's favorite word) to *tolerate*—the desire to insert my nipple into somebody's vagina. But with all my will power—and, like my mother's, it can be considerable when I marshal my forces—I was helpless once that bath began. Finally it was decided that nipple and areola should be sprayed with a mild anesthetic before Miss Clark started preparing me to meet the day. And this in fact did sufficiently reduce sensation so as to give me the upper hand in the battle against these impractical urges—a battle I won, however, only when the doctors decided, with my consent, to change my nurse.

That did the trick. Inserting my nipple into either the mouth or the anus of Mr. Brooks, the new male nurse, is something I just can't imagine with anything like the excitement I would imagine my nipple in Claire, or even in Miss Clark, though I realize that the conjunction of male mouth and female nipple can hardly be described as a homosexual act. But such is the power of my past and its taboos, and the power over my imagination of women and their apertures, that I am able now—temporarily anesthetized and in the hands of a man—to receive my morning ablutions like any other invalid, more or less.

And there is still Claire, angelic imperturbable Claire, to "make love" to me, with her mouth if not with her vagina. And isn't that sufficient? Isn't that incredible enough? Of course I dream of MORE, dream of it all day long—but what good is MORE to me anyway, when there is no orgasmic conclusion to my excitement, but only this sustained sense of imminent ejaculation in which I writhe from the first second to the last? Actually I have come by now to settle for less rather than MORE. I think I had better if I don't want Claire to come to see herself as nothing but the female machine summoned each evening to service a preposterous organism that once was David Kepesh. Surely the less time she spends at my nipple, the greater my chances of remaining something other to her (and to myself) than that nipple. Consequently, it is only for half of her hour-long visits that we now engage in sex—the rest of the time we spend in conversation. If I can, I should like to cut the sex play by half yet again.

If the excitement is always at the same pitch, neither increasing nor decreasing in intensity once it's begun, what's the difference if I experience it for fifteen rather than thirty minutes? What's the difference if it is for only *one* minute?

Mind you, I am not yet equal to such renunciation, nor am I convinced that it is desirable even from Claire's point of view. But it is something, I tell you, simply to entertain the idea after the torment I have known. Even now there are still moments, infrequent but searing, when I have all I can do not to cry out, while her lips are rhythmically palpating my nipple, "Fuck on it, Ovington! With your cunt!" But I don't, I don't. If Claire were of a mind to, she would have made the suggestion herself already. And, after all, she is still only a fourth-grade teacher at the Bank Street School, a girl brought up in Schenectady, New York, and Phi Beta Kappa at Cornell. No sense causing her to consider too carefully the grotesqueries she has already, miraculously, declared herself willing to participate in with the likes of me.

Sometime between the first and the second of the two major "crises" I have survived so far here in the hospital—if hospital it is—I was visited by Arthur Schonbrunn, Dean of Arts and Sciences at Stony Brook, and someone I have known since Palo Alto, when he was the young hot-shot Stanford professor and I was there getting my Ph.D. It was as the chairman of the newly formed comparative-literature department that Arthur brought me from Stanford to Stony Brook eight years ago. He is nearly fifty now, a wry and charming gentleman, and for an academic uncommonly, almost alarmingly, suave in manner and dress. It was his social expertise as much as our longstanding acquaintanceship that led me (and Dr. Klinger) to settle finally on Arthur as the best person with whom to make my social debut following the victory over the phallic cravings of my nipple. I also wanted Arthur to come so that I could talk to him—if not during this first visit, then the next—about how I might maintain my affiliation with the university. Back at Stanford I had been a "reader" for one of the enormous sophomore classes he lectured in "Masterpieces of Western Literature." I had begun to wonder if I couldn't perform some such function again. Claire could read aloud to me the student papers, I could dictate to her my comments and grades . . . Or was that a hopeless idea? It took Dr. Klinger several weeks to encourage me to believe that there would be no harm in asking.

I never got the chance. Even as I was telling him, a little "tearfully"—I couldn't help myself—how touched I was that he should be the first of my colleagues to visit, I thought I could hear giggling. "Arthur," I asked, "are we alone—?" He said, "Yes." Then giggled, quite distinctly. Sightless, I could still picture my former mentor: in his blue blazer with the paisley lining tailored in London for him by Kilgore, French; in his soft flannel trousers, in his gleaming Gucci loafers, the diplomatic Dean with his handsome mop of salt-and-pepper hair—giggling! And I hadn't even made my suggestion about becoming a reader for the department. Giggling—not because of anything ludicrous I had proposed, but because he saw that it was true, I actually *had* turned into a breast. My graduate-school adviser, my university superior, the most courtly professor I have ever known—and yet, from the sound of it, overcome with the giggles *simply at the sight of me.*

"I'm—I—David—" But now he was laughing so, he couldn't even speak. Arthur Schonbrunn unable to speak. Talk about the incredible. Twenty, thirty seconds more of uproarious laughter, and then he was gone. The visit had lasted about three minutes.

Two days later came the apology, as elegantly done, I'd say, as anything Arthur's written since his little book on Robert Musil. And the following week, the package from Sam Goody's, with a card signed, "Debbie and Arthur S." A record album of Laurence Olivier in *Hamlet.*

Arthur had written: "Your misfortune should

not have had to be compounded by my feeble, unforgivable performance. I'm at a loss to explain what came over me. It would strike us both as so much cant if I even tried."

I worked on my reply for a week. I must have dictated easily fifty letters: gracious, eloquent, forgiving, lighthearted, grave, hangdog, businesslike, arch, vicious, wild, literary—and some even sillier than the one I dispatched. "Feeble?" I wrote Arthur. "Why, if anything it is evidence of your earthly vitality that you should have laughed yourself sick. I am the feeble one, otherwise I would have joined in. If I fail to appreciate the enormous comedy of all this, it is only because I am really more of an Arthur Schonbrunn than you are, you vain, selfloving, dandified prick!" But the one I finally settled on read simply: "Dear Debbie and Arthur S.: Thanx mucho for the groovy sides. Dave 'The Breast' K." I checked twice with Claire to be sure she had spelled thanks with that x before she went ahead and mailed my little message. If she mailed it. If she even took it down.

The second crisis that threatened to undo me and that I appear—for the time being—to have weathered might be called a crisis of faith. As it came fully a month after Arthur's visit, it is hard to know if it was in any way precipitated by that humiliation. I am long since over hating Arthur Schonbrunn for that day—at least I continue to work at being long since over it—and so I tend now to agree with Dr. Klinger, who thinks that what I had to struggle with next was inevitable and can't be blamed on my three minutes with the Dean. Evidently nothing that has happened can be blamed on anyone, not even on me.

What happened next was that I refused to believe I had turned into a breast. Having brought myself to relinquish (more or less) my dreams of nippled intercourse with Claire, with Miss Clark—with whoever would have me—I realized that the whole thing was impossible. A man cannot turn into a breast other than in his own imagination.

It had taken me six months to figure this out.

"Look, this isn't happening—it can't!"

"Why can't it?" asked Dr. Klinger.

"You know why! Any child knows why! Because it is a physiological and biological and anatomical impossibility!"

"How then do you explain your predicament?"

"It's a dream! Six months haven't passed—that's an illusion, too. I'm dreaming! It's just a matter of waking up!"

"But you are awake, Mr. Kepesh. You know very well that you're awake."

"Stop saying that! Don't torture me like that! Let me get up! Enough! I want to wake up!"

For days and days—or what pass for days in a nightmare—I struggled to wake myself up. Claire came every evening to suck my nipple and talk, my father came on Sunday to tell me the latest news, Mr. Brooks was there every morning, rousing me from sleep with a gentle pat just at the edge of my areola. At least I imagined that he had just awakened me by touching the edge of my areola. Then I realized that I had not been awakened from a real sleep, but from the sleep that I slept within the nightmare itself. I wasn't an awakening breast—I was myself, still dreaming.

Oh, how I cursed my captors—though, to be sure, if it was a dream I was only cursing captors of my own invention. *Stop torturing me, all of you! Somebody help me get up!* I cursed the spectators in the gallery I had constructed, I cursed the technicians on the television circuit I had imagined—*Voyeurs!* I cried, *heartless, ogling, sadistic voyeurs!*—until at last, fearing that my battered system might collapse beneath the emotional strain (yes, those were the words of concern that I put into their lying mouths), they decided to place me under heavy sedation. How I howled then!—*Cold cunt of a Claire! Idiot, ignoramus of a father! Klinger you quack! Klinger you fraud!*—even as the drug enfeebled me, a sedating drug somehow administered to the dreamer by himself.

When I came around, I at last realized that I had gone mad. I was not dreaming. I was crazy. There was to be no magical awakening, no getting up out of bed, brushing my teeth, and going off to teach as though nothing more than a nightmare had interrupted my ordinary and predictable life; if there was ever to be anything at all for me, it was the long road back—becoming sane. And of course the first step toward recovering sanity was this realization that my sense of myself as a breast was the delusion of a lunatic, the realization that rather than being slung in a hammock following an endocrinopathic catastrophe unlike any the endocrinologists had ever known before, I was, more than likely, simply sitting, deluded, in a room in a mental hospital. And that is something we know can and does happen to all too many people, all the time. That I could not see, that I could not taste, that I could not smell, that I could only faintly hear, that I could not make contact with my own anatomy, that I experienced myself as speaking to others like one buried within, and very nearly strangulated by, his own adipose tissue—were these symptoms so unusual in the tranceworld of psychosis?

Why I had lost my sanity I couldn't understand, however. What could have triggered such a thoroughgoing schizophrenic collapse in someone seemingly so *well*? But then whatever might have caused such a breakdown was undoubtedly so frightening that I would have *had* to obliterate all memory of it . . . Only why then was Dr. Klinger—and that it was Dr. Klinger with whom I was talking I was sure; I had to be sure of something if I was to make a start, so I clung to his mildly accented English, to his straightforward manner and his homely humor as proof that at least *this* in my experience was real—why then was Dr. Klinger telling me to *accept* my fate, when clearly the way back to sanity was to *defy* this absolutely crazy conception of myself ? The answer was obvious—should have been all along! *That wasn't what Klinger was saying.* My illness was such that I was taking his words, simple and clear as they were when he spoke them, and giving them precisely the opposite meaning.

When he came that afternoon, I had to call forth all my famous strength of character in order to explain, as simply and clearly as I could, my incredible discovery. I sobbed when I was finished, but otherwise was as inspired in speech as I have ever been. When teaching, one sometimes hears oneself speaking in perfect cadences, developing ideas into rounded sentences, and combining them into paragraphs full to brimming, and it is hard then to believe that the fellow suddenly addressing his hushed students with a golden tongue and great decisiveness could have made such a muddle of his notes only the hour before. Well, harder still to believe that the measured tones in which I had just broken the good news to Dr. Klinger came from the vituperous madman who had to be sedated only the day before by his keepers. If I was still a lunatic—and still a breast, I was still a lunatic—I was now, at least, one of the more lucid and eloquent on my floor.

I said, "Curiously, it's Arthur Schonbrunn's visit that convinces me I'm on the right track. How could I ever have believed that Arthur would come here and *laugh*? How could I take that blatantly paranoid delusion for the truth? I've been cursing him for a month now—and Debbie too, for those idiotic records—and none of it makes any sense at all. Because if there is one person in the world who simply *couldn't* lose control like that, it's Arthur."

"He is beyond the perils of human nature, this Dean?"

"You know something? The answer to that is yes. He is beyond the perils of human nature."

"Such a shrewd operator."

"It isn't that he's so shrewd—that's going at it the wrong way round. It's that I've been so mad. To think that I actually made all that up!"

"And his note, which you answered so graciously? The note that made you so livid?"

"More paranoia."

"And the recording of *Hamlet*?"

"Ah, *that's* Mr. Reality. That is real—and right up Debbie's alley. Oh yes, I can feel the difference now, even as I talk I can sense the difference between the insane stuff and what's truly happened. Oh, I do feel the difference, *you must believe me*. I've gone mad, but now I know it!"

"And what do you think caused you, as you put it, to 'go mad'?" Dr. Klinger asked.

"I don't remember."

"Any idea at all? What could have drawn someone like you into such a fully developed and impenetrable delusion?"

"I'm telling you the truth, Doctor. I don't have the least idea. Not yet, anyway."

"Nothing comes to mind? Nothing at all?"

"Well, what comes to mind, if anything—what came to mind this morning—"

"Is what?"

"I'm grasping at straws—and I know how whimsical it seems in the circumstances. But I thought, 'I got it from fiction.' The books I've been teaching—they put the idea in my head. I'm thinking of my European Literature course. Teaching Gogol and Kafka every year—teaching 'The Nose' and 'Metamorphosis.' "

"Of course, many other literature professors teach 'The Nose' and 'Metamorphosis.' "

"But maybe," said I, the humor intentional now, "not with so much conviction."

He laughed.

"I *am* mad, though—aren't I?" I asked.

"No."

I was set back only momentarily. I realized that I had inverted his meaning as easily, and as unconsciously, as we turn right side up the images that flash upon the retina upside down.

"I want to tell you," I calmly explained, "that though you just answered yes when I asked whether I was mad, I heard you say no."

"I did say no. You are not mad. You are not suffering from a delusion—or certainly haven't been, up till now. You are a breast, of sorts. You have been heroic in your efforts to accommodate yourself to a mysterious misfortune. Of course one understands the temptation: this is all just a dream, a hallucination, a delusion—even a drug-induced state of mind. But, in fact, it is none of these things. It is something that has happened to you. And the best way to go mad—do you hear me, Mr. Kepesh?—*the way into madness* is to start to pretend otherwise. The comfort of that will be short-lived, I can assure you. I want you right now to disabuse yourself of the notion that you are insane. You are not insane, and to pretend to be insane will only bring you to grief. Insanity is no solution—neither imagined insanity nor the real thing."

"Again I heard everything reversed. I turned the sense of your words completely around."

"No, you did not."

"*Does* it make any sense to you to think of my delusion as somehow fueled by years of teaching those stories? I mean, regardless of the trauma that triggered the breakdown itself."

"But there was no trauma, not of a psychological nature; and as I have told you, and tell you now again, and will continue to tell you: *this is no delusion.*"

How to press on? How to break through this reversing?

With an artfulness that pleased me—and bespoke health! health!—I said, "But if it were, Dr. Klinger—since I again understood you to say just the opposite of what you said—*if* it were, would you *then* see any connection between the kind of hallucination I've embedded myself in and the power over my imagination of Kafka or Gogol? Or of Swift? I'm thinking of *Gulliver's Travels*, another book I've taught for years. Perhaps if we go on speaking hypothetically—"

"Mr. Kepesh, enough. You are fooling no one but yourself—if even yourself. There has been shock, panic, fury, despair, disorientation, profound feelings of helplessness and isolation, the darkest depression and fear, but through it all, quite miraculously, quite marvelously, no delusions. Not even when your old friend the Dean showed up and had his laughing fit. Of course that shocked you. Of course that crushed you. Why shouldn't it have? But you did not imagine Arthur Schonbrunn's unfortunate behavior. You have not made up what has happened to you, and you did not make up what happened here to him. You didn't have to. You are pretending to be a naïf, you know, when you tell me that such a reaction is simply out of the question for a man in Arthur Schonbrunn's position. You are a better student of human nature than that. You've read too much Dostoevsky for that."

"Will it help if I repeat to you what I thought I heard you say?"

"No need. What you thought you heard, you heard. That is known as sanity. Come off the lunatic kick, Mr. Kepesh—and the sooner the better. Gogol, Kafka, and so on—it is going to get you into serious trouble if you keep it up. The next thing you know you will have produced in yourself genuine and irreversible delusions exactly like those you now claim to want to be rid of. Do you follow me? I think you do. You are a highly intelligent man and you have a remarkably strong will, and I want you to stop it right now."

How exhausting to hear it all backwards! How ingenious insanity is! But at least I *knew*. "Dr. Klinger! Dr. Klinger! Listen to me—I won't let it drive me crazy any more! I will fight myself free! I will stop hearing the opposite! I will start hearing what you are all saying! Do you hear *me*, Doctor? Do you understand *my* words? I will not participate any longer in this delusion! I refuse to be a part of it! You *will* get through to me! I *will* understand what you mean! Just don't give up! Please," I pleaded, "don't give me up for lost! I will break through and be myself again! I am determined! With all my strength—with all my will to live!"

Now I spent my days trying to penetrate the words I heard so as to get through to what actually was being said to me by the doctors, and by Claire, and by Mr. Brooks. The effort this required was so total, and so depleting, that by nightfall I felt it would take no more than a puff from a child's lips to extinguish for good the wavering little flame of memory and intelligence and hope still claiming to be me.

When my father came for his Sunday visit, I told him everything, even though I was sure that Claire and Klinger would have let him know by phone the day it happened. I babbled like a boy who'd won a trophy. It was true, I told him—I no longer believed I was a breast. If I had not yet been able to throw off the physical sense of unreality, I was daily divesting myself of the preposterous psychic delusion; every day, every hour I sensed myself slowly turning back into myself, and could even begin to see through to the time when I would again be teaching Gogol and Kafka rather than experiencing vicariously the unnatural transformations they had imagined in their famous fictions. Since my father knows nothing of books, I told him how Gregor Samsa awakens in the Kafka story to discover that he has become an enormous beetle; I summarized for him "The Nose," recounting how Gogol's hero awakens one morning missing his nose, how he sets out to look for it in St. Petersburg, places an ad in the newspaper requesting its return, sees "it" walking on the street, one ridiculous encounter after another, until in the end the nose just turns up again on his face for no better reason than it disappeared. (I could imagine my father thinking, "He teaches this stuff, in a college?") I explained that I still couldn't remember the blow that had done me in; I actually became deaf, *could not hear*, when the doctor tried to get me to face it. But whatever the trauma itself may have been—however terrifying, horrifying, repellent—what I knew was that my escape route was through the fantasy of physical transformation that lay immediately at hand, the catastrophe stories by Kafka and Gogol that I had been teaching my students only the week before. Now, with Dr. Klinger's assistance, I was trying to figure out just why, of all things, I had chosen a breast. Why a big brainless bag of dumb, desirable tissue, acted upon instead of acting, unguarded, immobile, hanging, *there*, as a breast simply hangs and is *there*? Why this primitive identification with *the* object of infantile veneration? What unfulfilled appetites, what cradle confusions, what fragments out of my remotest past could have collided to spark a delusion of such classical simplicity? On and on I babbled to my father, and then, once again, joyously, I wept. No tears, but I wept. Where *were* my tears? How soon before I would feel tears again? When would I feel my teeth, my tongue, my toes?

For a long while my father said nothing. I thought that perhaps he was crying too. Then he went into the weekly news report: so-and-so's daughter is pregnant, so-and-so's son has bought himself a hundred-thousand-dollar home, my uncle is catering Richard Tucker's younger brother's son's wedding.

He hadn't even heard me. Of course. I may have broken through the *idea* that I was a breast, but I still seemed required virtually to give a recitation, as from a stage, if I wanted to make myself understood. What I believed was a normal conversational tone tended, apparently, to come out sounding like somebody muttering across the room. But this wasn't because my voice box was buried in a hundred-and-fifty-five-pound mammary gland. My body was still a body! I had only to stop whispering! I had only to speak out! Could that be part of the madness? That when I believed I was speaking aloud, I was speaking only to myself? Speak up then!

And so I did. At the top of my lungs (my two good lungs!) repeated to my father the story of my breakthrough.

And then it was time to take the next step. One foot in front of the other. "Dad," I said, "where are we? You tell me."

"In your room," he answered.

"And tell me, have I turned into a breast?"

"Well, that's what they say."

"But that's not true. I'm a mental patient. Now tell me again—what am I?"

"Oh, Davey."

"*What am I?*"

"You're a woman's breast."

"That's not true! What I heard you say is not true! I'm a mental patient! In a hospital! And you are visiting me! Dad, if that's the truth, I just want you to say yes. Listen to me now. You must help me. I am a mental patient. I am in a mental hospital. I have had a severe mental breakdown. Yes or no. *Tell me the truth.*"

And my father answered, "Yes, son, yes. You're a mental patient."

"I heard him!" I cried to Klinger when he came later in the day. "I heard my father! I heard the truth! I heard him say I'm a mental patient!"

"He should never have told you that."

"I heard it! I'm not imagining it either! It didn't get reversed!"

"Of course you heard it. Your father loves you.

He's a simple man and he loves you very much. He thought it would help if he said it. He knows now that it can't. And so do you."

But I couldn't have been happier. My father had gotten through to me. I could be gotten through to! It would follow with the others soon enough. "I heard it!" I said. "I'm not a breast! I'm mad!"

How I strain in the coming days to be my sane self again! How I dredge at the muck of my beginnings, searching for what will explain—and thus annihilate—this preposterous delusion! I have returned, I tell the doctor, to the dawn of my life, to my first thousand hours after the eons of hours of nothing—back to when all is oneself and oneself is all, back to when the concave is the convex and the convex the concave . . . oh, how I talk! How I work to outsmart my madness! If I could only remember my hungering gums at the spigot of love, my nose in the nourishing globe—! "Oh, if she were alive, if she could tell me—" "Yes? Tell you what?" asks Klinger. "Oh," I moan, "how do *I* know?" But where else to begin but there? Only there there is nothing. It is all *too* far back, back where I am. To dive to that sea bottom where I began—to find in the slime this secret! But when I rise to the surface, there is not even silt beneath my fingernails. I come up with nothing.

Perhaps, I say, perhaps, I tell him, it is all a post-analytic collapse, a year in the making—the most desperate means I could devise to cling to Klinger. "Have you ever thought what fantasies of dependence bloom in your patients merely on the basis of your name? Have you realized, Doctor, that all *our* names begin with K, yours and mine and Kafka's? And then there is Claire—and Miss Clark!" "The alphabet," he reminds me, a language teacher, "only *has* twenty-six letters. And there are four billion of us in need of initials for purposes of identification." "But!" "But what?" "But *something*! But *anything*! Please, a clue! If I can't—then *you*. Please, some clue, some lead—I have to get out!"

I go over with him again the salient moments in my psychological development, once again I turn the pages in the anthology of stories that we two had assembled as text for the course conducted by us, three times a week for five years, in

"The History of David Alan Kepesh." But in fact those stories have been recounted and glossed so exhaustively so many times that they are as stale to me as the favorite literary chestnut of the most retrograde schoolteacher in America. My life's drama, as exciting in the early years of therapy as *The Brothers Karamazov*, has all the appeal now of some tenth-grade reader beginning with "The Necklace" and running through to "The Luck of Roaring Camp." Which accounts for the successful termination of analysis the year before.

And *there*, I thought, is my trauma! Success itself ! There is what I couldn't take—a happy life! "What is that?" asks Dr. Klinger quizzically. "What was it you couldn't take?" "Rewards—instead of punishment! Wholeness! Comfort! Pleasure! A gratifying way of life, a life *without*—" "Wait just a minute, please. Why couldn't you take such things? Those are wonderful things. Come off it, Mr. Kepesh. As I remember, you could take happiness with the best of them." But I refuse to listen, since what I hear him saying isn't what he's saying anyway. That is just my illness, turning things around to keep me insane. On I go instead, talking next about what patients will talk about sooner or later—that imaginary friend they call My Guilt. I talk about Helen, my former wife, whose life, I have been told, is no better now than when we suffered together through five years of that marriage. I remember I couldn't help but gloat a little when I heard about Helen's continuing unhappiness from an old San Francisco friend, who had come to dinner with me and my lovely, imperturbable Claire. Good for the bitch, I thought . . . "And now," Klinger asks with amusement, "you believe you are punishing yourself in this way for such ordinary, everyday malice?" "I'm saying that my happy new life was too much for me! It's why I lost my desire for Claire—it was all too good to last! So much satisfaction seemed—seemed unjust! Compared to Helen's fate, seemed somehow iniquitous! My Guilt!" I plead. "My dear sir," he replies, "that is analysis right out of the dime store—and you know it as well as I do." "Then if not that, *what?* Help me! Tell me! *What did it?*"

"Nothing 'did it.' "

"*Then why in God's name am I mad?*"

"But you're not. And you know that too."

The next Sunday, when he comes to visit, I

again ask my father if I am a mental patient—just to be sure—and this time he answers, "No."

"*But last week you said yes!*"

"I was wrong."

"*But it's the truth!*"

"It's not."

"I'm reversing again! I've lost it now with you! I'm back where I was! I'm reversing with everyone!"

"You're not at all," said Dr. Klinger.

"What are you doing here? This is Sunday! My father is here, not you! You're not even here!"

"I'm here. With your father. Right beside you, the two of us."

"This is getting all crazy again! I don't want to be crazy any more! Help me! Do you hear me? Am I being heard? Help me, please! I need your help! I cannot do this alone! Help me! Lift me! Tell me only the truth! If I am a breast, where is my milk! When Claire is sucking me, where is the milk! Tell me *that*!"

"Oh, David." It was my father, his unshaven cheek on my areola! "My son, my poor sonny."

"Oh, Daddy, what's happened? Hold me,

Poppy, please. What's really happened? Tell me, please, *why did I go mad?*"

"You didn't, darling," he sobbed.

"*Then where is my milk? Answer me! If I am a breast I would make milk! Hold milk! Swell with milk! And that is too crazy for anybody to believe! Even me! THAT SIMPLY CANNOT BE!*"

But evidently it can be. Just as they are able to increase the milk yield of cows with injections of the lactogenic agent GH, the growth hormone, so it has been hypothesized that I very likely could become a milk-producing mammary gland with appropriate hormonal stimulation. If so, there must be those out in the scientific world who would jump at the chance to find out. And when I have had my fill of all this, perhaps I will give it to them. And if I am not killed in the process? If they succeed and milk begins to flow? Well, then I will know that I am indeed a wholly authentic breast—or else that I am as mad as any man has ever been.

In the meantime fifteen months have passed—by their calendar—and I live for the moment in relative equanimity. That is, things have been worse and will be again, but for now, for now Claire still comes to visit every day, does not miss a single day, and still, for the first half hour of each hour, uncomplainingly and without repugnance attends to my pleasure. Converts a disgusting perversion into a kindly, thoughtful act of love. And then we talk. She is helping me with my Shakespeare studies. I have been listening of late to recordings of the tragedies. I began with the Schonbrunns' gift, Olivier in *Hamlet*. The album lay for months here in the room before I asked Mr. Brooks one morning to break the cellophane wrapper and put a record on the phonograph. (Mr. Brooks turns out to be a Negro; and so, in my mind's eye—a breast's mind's eye, to be sure—I imagine him looking like the handsome black Senator from Massachusetts. Why not, if it makes this cozier for me?) Like so many people, I have been meaning ever since college to sit down someday and reread Shakespeare. I may even once have said as much to Debbie Schonbrunn, and she bought the record album because she realized that I now had the time. Surely no satire was ever intended, however much I may have believed otherwise when the *Hamlet* arrived the week after Arthur's three-minute visit. I must remember that aside from the more obvious difficulties occasioned by my transformation, I am no longer the easiest person in the world to buy a present for.

For several hours every morning and again sometimes in the afternoons when there is nothing better to do, I listen to my Shakespeare records: Olivier playing Hamlet and Othello, Paul Scofield as Lear, *Macbeth* as performed by the Old Vic company. Unable to follow with a text while the play is being spoken, I invariably miss the meaning of an unfamiliar word, or lose my way in the convoluted syntax, and then my mind begins to wander, and when I tune in again, little makes sense for lines on end. Despite the effort—oh, the effort, minute-by-minute this effort!—to keep my attention fixed on the plight of Shakespeare's suffering heroes, I do continue to consider my own suffering more than can be good for me.

The Shakespeare edition I used in college—Neilson and Hill, *The Complete Plays and Poems of William Shakespeare*, bound in blue linen, worn at the spine by my earnest undergraduate grip, and heavily underlined by me then for wisdom—is on the table beside the hammock. It is one of several books I have asked Claire to bring from my apartment. I remember exactly what it looks like, which in part is why I wanted it here. In the evenings, during the second half hour of her visit, Claire looks up for me in the footnotes words whose usage I long ago learned and forgot; or she will slowly read aloud some passage that I missed that morning when my mind departed Elsinore Castle for Lenox Hill Hospital. It seems to me important to get these passages clear in my head—my brain—before I go off to sleep. Otherwise it might begin to seem that I listen to *Hamlet* for the same reason that my father answers the phone at my Uncle Larry's catering establishment—to kill time.

Olivier is a great man, you know. I have fallen in love with him a little, like a schoolgirl with a movie star. I've never before given myself over to a genius so completely, not even while reading. As a student, as a professor, I experienced literature as something unavoidably tainted by my self-consciousness and all the responsibilities of serious discourse; either I was learning or I was teaching. But responsibilities are behind me now; at last I can just listen.

In the beginning I used to try to amuse myself when I was alone in the evenings by imitating Olivier. I worked with my records during the day to memorize the famous soliloquies, and then I performed for myself at night, trying to approximate his distinctive delivery. After some weeks it seemed to me that I had really rather mastered his Othello, and one night, after Claire had left,

I did the death-scene speech with such plaintive passion that I thought I could have moved an audience to tears. Until I realized that I had an audience. It was midnight, or thereabouts, but nobody has given me a good reason yet why the TV camera should shut down at any hour of the day or night—and so I left off with my performance. Enough pathos is enough, if not, generally, too much. "Come now, David," said I to myself, "it is all too poignant and heartbreaking, a breast reciting 'And say besides, that in Aleppo once . . . ' You will send the night shift home in tears." Yes, bitterness, dear reader, and of a shallow sort, but then permit my poor professorial dignity a little rest, won't you? This is not tragedy any more than it is farce. It is only life, and I am only human.

Did fiction do this to me? "How could it have?" asks Dr. Klinger. "No, hormones are hormones and art is art. You are not suffering from an overdose of the great imaginations." "Aren't I? I wonder. This might well be my way of being a Kafka, being a Gogol, being a Swift. They could envision the incredible, they had the words and those relentless fictionalizing brains. But I had neither, I had nothing—literary longings and that was it. I loved the extreme in literature, idolized those who wrote it, was virtually hypnotized by the imagery and the power—" "And? Yes? The world is full of art lovers—so?" "So I took the leap. Made the word flesh. Don't you see, I have out-Kafkaed Kafka." Klinger laughed, as though I meant to be only amusing. "After all," I said, "who is the greater artist, he who imagines the marvelous transformation, or he who marvelously transforms himself ? Why David Kepesh? Why me, of all people, endowed with such powers? Simple. Why Kafka? Why Gogol? Why Swift? Why anyone? Great art happens to people like anything else. And this is my great work of art! Ah," but I quickly added, "I must maintain my sane and reasonable perspective. I don't wish to upset you again. No delusions—delusions of grandeur least of all."

But if not grandeur, what about abasement? What about depravity and vice? I could be rich, you know, I could be rich, notorious, and delirious with pleasure every waking hour of the day.

I think about it more and more. I could call my friend to visit me, the adventurous younger colleague I spoke of earlier. If I haven't dared to invite him yet, it isn't because I'm frightened that he'll laugh and run like Arthur Schonbrunn, but rather that he'll take one look at what I am—and what I could be—and be all too eager to help; that when I tell him I have had just about enough of being a heroically civilized fellow about it all, enough of listening to Olivier and talking to my analyst and enjoying thirty minutes every day of some virtuous schoolteacher's idea of hot sex, he won't argue, the way others would. "I want to get out of here," I'll say to him, "and I need an accomplice. We can carry with us all the pumps and pipes that sustain me. And to look after my health, such as it is, we can hire the doctors and nurses to come along—money will be no problem. But I am sick and tired of worrying about losing Claire. Let her go and find a new lover whose sperm she will not drink, and lead with him a normal and productive life. I am tired of guarding against the loss of her angelic goodness. And between the two of us, I am a little tired of my old man too—he bores me.

And, really, how much Shakespeare do you think I can take? I wonder if you realize how many of the great plays of Western literature are now available on excellent long-playing records. When I finish with Shakespeare, I can go right on to first-rate performances of Sophocles, Sheridan, Aristophanes, Shaw, Racine—but to what end? To what end! That *is* killing time. For a breast it is the bloody *murder* of time. Pal, I am going to make a pot of money. I don't think it should be difficult, either. If the Beatles can fill Shea Stadium, why can't I? We will have to think this through, you and I, but then what was all that education for, if not to learn to think things through? To read more books? To write more critical essays? Further contemplation of the higher things? How about some contemplation of the lower? I will make hundreds of thousands of dollars—and then I will have girls, twelve- and thirteen-year-old girls, three, four, and five at a time, naked and giggling, and all on my nipple at once. I want them for days on end, greedy wicked little girls, licking me and sucking me to my heart's content. And we can find them, you know that. If the Rolling Stones can find them, if Charles Manson can find them, then with all our education we can probably find a few ourselves. And women. There will also be women quite eager to open their thighs to a cock as new and thrilling as my nipple. I think we will be happily surprised by the number of respectable women who will come knocking at the dressing-room door in their respectable chinchillas just to get a peek at the tint of my soft hermaphroditic flesh. Well, we will have to be discriminating, won't we, we will have to select from among them according to beauty, good breeding, and the lewdness of their desire. And I will be deliriously happy. *And I will be deliriously happy.* Remember Gulliver among the Brobdingnags? How the maidservants had him strolling out on their nipples for the fun of it? He didn't think it was fun, poor lost little man. But then he was a humane English physician, a child of the Age of Reason, a faithful follower of the Sense of Proportion trapped on a continent of outlandish giants; but this, my friend and accomplice, is the Land of Opportunity, this is the Age of Self-Fulfillment, and I am the Breast, and will live by my own lights!"

"Live by them or die by them?"

"It remains to be seen, Dr. Klinger."

Permit me now to conclude my lecture by quoting the poet Rilke. As a passionately well-meaning literature teacher I was always fond of ending the hour with something moving for the students to carry from the uncontaminated classroom out into the fallen world of junk food and pop stars and dope. True, Kepesh's occupation's gone—*Othello*, Act III, Scene 3—but I haven't lost entirely a teacher's good intentions. Maybe I haven't even lost my students. On the basis of my fame, I may even have acquired vast new flocks of undergraduate sheep, as innocent of calamity as of verse. I may even be a pop star now myself and have just what it takes to bring great poetry to the people.

("Your fame?" says Dr. Klinger. "Surely the world knows by now," I say, "excepting perhaps the Russians and Chinese." "In accordance with your wishes, the case has been handled with the utmost discretion." "But my friends know. The staff here knows. That's enough of a start for something like this." "True. But by the time the news filters beyond those who know and out to the man in the street, he tends by and large not to believe it." "He thinks it's a joke." "If he can take his mind off his own troubles long enough to think anything at all." "And the media? You're suggesting they've done nothing with this either?" "Nothing at all." "I don't buy that, Dr. Klinger." "Don't. I'm not going to argue. I told you long ago—there of course were inquiries in the beginning. But nothing was done to assist anyone, and after a while these people have a living to make like everybody else, and they move right along to the next promising misfortune." "Then no one knows all that's happened." "All? No one but you knows it all, Mr. Kepesh." "Well, maybe I should be the one to tell all then." "Then you *will* be famous, won't you?" "Better the truth than tabloid fantasy. Better from me than from the chattering madmen and morons." "Of course the madmen and the morons will chatter anyway, you know. You realize that you will never be taken on your own terms, regardless of what you say." "I'll still be a joke." "A joke. A freak. If you insist on being the one to tell them, a charlatan too." "You're advising me to leave well enough alone. You're advising me to keep this all to myself." "I'm advising you nothing, only reminding you of our friend with the beard who sits on the throne." "Mr. Reality." "And his principle," says Klinger.)

And now to conclude the hour with the poem by Rainer Maria Rilke entitled "Archaic Torso of Apollo" written in Paris in 1908. Perhaps my story, told here in its entirety for the first time, and with all the truthfulness that's in me, will at the very least illuminate these great lines for those of you new to the poem—particularly the poet's concluding admonition, which may not be so elevated a sentiment as appears at first glance. Morons and madmen, tough guys and skeptics, friends, students, relatives, colleagues, and all you distracted strangers, with your billion different fingerprints and faces—my fellow mammalians, let us proceed with our education, one and all.

The Breast

We did not know his legendary head,
in which the eyeballs ripened. But
his torso still glows like a candelabrum
in which his gaze, only turned low,

holds and gleams. Else could not the curve
of the breast blind you, nor in the slight turn
of the loins could a smile be running
to that middle, which carried procreation.

Else would this stone be standing maimed and short
under the shoulders' translucent plunge
nor flimmering like the fell of beasts of prey

nor breaking out of all its contours
like a star: for there is no place
that does not see you. You must change your life.

Printed in the United States
by Baker & Taylor Publisher Services